Reality Check

Adapted by N. B. Grace

Based on the series created by Michael Poryes and Rich Correll & Barry O'Brien

Part One is based on the episode, "Song Sung Bad," Written by Ingrid Escajeda

Part Two is based on the episode, "Sleepwalk This Way," Written by Heather Wordham

Disney PRESS

New York

Printed in the United States of America

First Edition
1 3 5 7 9 10 8 6 4 2

Library of Congress Control Number: 2009902702
ISBN 978-1-4231-1424-6

For more Disney Press fun, visit www.disneybooks.com
Visit DisneyChannel.com

PART ONE

Chapter One

Hannah Montana was in the recording studio, belting out her latest hit. Her best friend, Lola Luftnagle, was sitting in the sound booth, bopping along to the beat. Hannah's manager sat next to Lola, smiling in approval as he listened to Hannah sing. It was just another day in the life of an international pop star . . .

Except that in reality, Hannah was regular fifteen-year-old high school student

Miley Stewart. She had been transformed into her pop star persona by a fashionable outfit, makeup, and a long blond wig that covered her brown hair. Hannah's best friend, Lola, was really Miley's best friend, Lilly Truscott. As usual, Lilly was wearing a short, colorful wig to help hide her true identity. Today's pick was purple. And Hannah's manager—the guy with the mustache and cowboy hat sitting at the control panel—was really Miley's dad, Robby Ray Stewart.

They were all disguised because Hannah Montana's real identity was a closely guarded secret. Only Miley's brother, Jackson, and her other best friend, Oliver Oken, knew the truth.

Sometimes it was tough for Miley to play the part of both pop sensation and down-to-earth teenager. She had gotten into plenty of scrapes as she tried to juggle her celebrity life and her normal life. But at moments like this, when she was able to enjoy her true love—singing—she felt it was all worthwhile.

"Man, Miley is so lucky," Lilly commented. "Her voice is so pure and natural and . . ."

As she spoke, Lilly leaned forward, accidentally causing some of the levers on the sound board to slide. Miley's upbeat singing voice suddenly turned into a horrible growl.

Miley frowned as she took her headphones off. "There is *no* way that's me."

She could see her dad through the window in the booth of the recording studio, nodding in agreement. "Uh, Lola . . ." he said, turning to Miley's friend.

"Oh! Sorry!" Lilly exclaimed, blushing as she realized what she had done. "My bad."

Quickly, she tried to readjust the levers, but this only created horrible feedback. The sound shrieked through the room, startling Miley so much that she fell off her chair.

After taking a few seconds to catch her breath, Miley got up, put her headphones back on, and finished singing the last line of the song, giving one final "Whoa-oh, yeah!" at the end. "How'd that sound, Dad?" she said into her microphone.

"Perfect," Mr. Stewart answered, smiling.

Lilly bounded into the recording studio from the control room. "That is such a great song!" she gushed. "Have I told you it's my mom's favorite?"

Miley gave her friend a curious look. Lilly was not the gushing type. Something was definitely going on. And Miley had a feeling that Lilly was working herself up to ask for a favor.

Sure enough, Lilly continued. "Hey, here's a wacky idea! Her birthday's coming up. Maybe you could make a special, kind of personal recording and I could give it to her as a present?" Lilly suggested, trying to sound nonchalant.

Of course, Miley thought. I should have seen this coming! They had gone to the mall the other day so that Lilly could look for a present for her mom. They had shopped for hours, but Miley now realized that Lilly hadn't actually bought a present.

"You spent all her gift money on those shoes, didn't you?" Miley said, remembering the heels Lilly had bought.

Lilly looked down guiltily. "They didn't have them in her size," she protested weakly.

But she didn't have to explain herself to her best friend. "I hear you," Miley said. She tossed her head so Lilly could get a good look at the cute jewelry dangling from her ears. "Last Christmas, I bought Daddy these earrings."

Lilly laughed, relieved that they were so much alike. "See? This is why we're friends."

"Exactly," Miley agreed, smiling.

"So, you'll do it?" Lilly asked eagerly. "You'll record the song?"

"Nope," Miley said. "*You* will."

Lilly laughed again. That Miley! Always joking around! But she stopped laughing when she saw the look on Miley's face. "You're not kidding."

"No, kidding's when I tell my dad that he looks good in that dorky mustache," Miley said, nodding toward Mr. Stewart. He always wore a fake mustache as part of his disguise. It did look a little odd, but he was very proud of it.

"Your mic's still on, darlin'," Mr. Stewart said into his microphone.

"Love you!" Miley shouted cheerfully. She turned back to her friend. "Lilly, to make this special, *you're* going to have to record the song."

"But I don't have a voice like yours," Lilly said worriedly.

"You'll be surprised what you can sound like in a professional studio," Miley told her. "Trust me, you're going to sound great."

Lilly hesitated. She was really good at some things, like skateboarding, surfing, and soccer. She was okay at other things, like playing video games and cooking. And then she was . . . well, still working on some skills, like taking geometry tests and singing.

But she shrugged. After all, Miley wasn't

just Miley. She was Hannah Montana! If *she* didn't know about recording a song, who would?

"Okay," Lilly said slowly. She stepped up to the mic and took a deep breath. Then she began to sing the lyrics Miley had just recorded.

Miley tried to keep a smile on her face, but only because she was trying so hard not to show how stunned she was. Lilly's singing was pretty bad!

Miley glanced over at her dad. His mouth was hanging open in shock.

Lilly finished the song, beaming. Clearly, she had no idea how she really sounded.

"So, you think my mom will like it?" she asked Miley excitedly.

"*Like* it?" Miley asked. "She's going to be speechless. Right, Dad?"

But Mr. Stewart was already speechless

after listening to Lilly sing. "Uh . . . uh . . ." he stuttered.

Miley nodded at Lilly. "You see?"

Lilly continued smiling. But Miley was concerned. *Oh, no,* she thought. *This is so not good.*

Chapter Two

Later that day, Miley was back home, sitting at the kitchen table with her friend Oliver. They had just finished listening to Lilly's recording.

Oliver appeared just as horrified by what he had heard as Miley had been at the recording studio.

"You're not actually going to give this to her, are you?" he asked with concern.

"Of course not," Miley replied. "I'm

going to give her *this* one."

She popped another CD into the stereo and hit a button. Lilly's voice filled the room once more . . . but this time it sounded great!

"Wow," Oliver commented, his eyes widening in surprise. "A little reverb, some overlay. Nice!"

Miley smiled with satisfaction. "Daddy called it 'Extreme Mix-Over: Lilly Edition.' Now she'll never know how unbelievably—"

Just then, Lilly bounded into the living room, dressed in the athletic clothes she usually wore. "Hi, hi," she called out.

"Wonderful she is!" Miley finished, thinking fast. She beamed at Lilly. "Listen to you, you singer, you!"

She hit the PLAY button again. Lilly's mouth dropped open in amazement.

"Oh, my gosh!" she exclaimed. "I'm fantastic!"

"Almost too good to believe," Oliver said pointedly. Miley stomped on his foot. Wincing, he added quickly, "But not!"

"My mom is going to be so blown away," Lilly said happily. "I have to tell you, I was a little nervous. Nobody in my family can really sing," she confessed to Miley.

Miley handed Lilly the headphones. "Hey, why don't you just, uh, listen through the headphones? You know, get the full effect."

As Lilly listened to herself on the CD, she got so carried away that she started singing along. Loudly. In a voice that was almost screeching and definitely, horribly off-key.

Lilly glanced at her friends to see their reaction. They both smiled and waved at her. Unaware of the pain she was causing her audience, Lilly kept singing and swaying to the music, a blissful look on her face.

Seeing how happy her friend was, Miley knew she had done the right thing. And she had done it so well that Lilly would never, ever find out . . . or so Miley hoped.

Chapter Three

That same afternoon, Miley's brother, Jackson, was at the Surf Shack, a beach-side snack stand where he worked part-time. The Surf Shack was owned by the father of a kid named Rico, who was in Miley's grade because he had skipped a few years of school.

Rico was Jackson's worst nightmare. Just because his dad was Jackson's boss, he thought he could order Jackson around.

As far as Jackson was concerned, a day without Rico was a beautiful day indeed.

So Jackson's heart sank when he looked up from cleaning the counter to see Rico approaching. He was wearing a costume that made him look like a cross between a matador and a flamenco dancer. He was also wearing a fake mustache. In other words, he looked ridiculous.

But even though he was younger and shorter than everyone else in his grade, Rico wore the bold costume with pride. When he saw a girl staring at him, he struck a pose.

"Yeah," he said, nodding grandly. "Go ahead and look, but you can't touch."

"Dude, what happened to you?" Jackson asked, trying not to laugh. "Did you get lost on the way to a bullfight?"

"Go ahead and joke, but my father won

my mother's heart dressed like this," Rico said.

Jackson shook his head at this logic. "Your father's a billionaire," he pointed out. "He could've dressed like a duck and won her heart." He leaned in a little closer to examine Rico's face. "And what died on your lip?" he asked, reaching out to touch Rico's mustache.

Rico pulled away, embarrassed. He glanced over at a group of girls nearby. "Stop it!" he hissed to Jackson. "She'll see."

He nodded toward a girl who was sitting on a mat, doing a yoga pose. Her eyes were closed and her expression was very calm.

Jackson raised his eyebrows in surprise. He knew that girl. Her name was Sarah and she was in Miley and Rico's grade. She was known as "Saint Sarah" for her do-good ways and her determination to save the world.

"This is all for *Sarah*?" Jackson asked incredulously. "Oh, come on, Rico, what did that poor girl ever do to you?"

"She stole my heart!" Rico said dramatically. Then a crafty look appeared in his eyes. "I just wish I had someone who could find out if she likes me, too. A friend, a pal"—he gave Jackson a meaningful glance—"an easily replaceable employee."

It was clear who Rico was referring to. Jackson thought about refusing. After all, he didn't work for Rico. He wasn't friends with Rico. He should just tell Rico to get lost.

But then he had second thoughts. He knew from experience that Rico could make a guy's life miserable. He was very creative that way.

"All right, fine," Jackson said. "But lose the 'stache!" Then he sighed and walked over to Sarah. "Hey, Sarah. Nice pose," he said to her.

"Thanks," Sarah said brightly. "It aligns my chakras."

Jackson had to restrain himself from rolling his eyes. He thought people that did yoga were so weird!

"Well, you're going to be in for *chakra*"—as a joke, Jackson pronounced it *shock-ra*—"when you hear what I have to say."

Sarah's face lit up with anticipation. She jumped up from her mat. "The president got my letter and agreed to give Arizona back to the Apaches?"

Jackson heaved a deep sigh. Sometime he'd like to visit the dream world Sarah lived in. It was so bizarrely different from the real world. But right now, he had a job to do. "This'll go a lot faster if you just stop talking," he said.

"Okay," Sarah said, nodding.

"Look," Jackson said. He put his arm around her shoulders and began slowly leading her in Rico's direction. "There's this guy who really likes you, but he's kind of shy and he doesn't want to say anything until he knows whether you like him, too."

"Oh, my gosh!" Sarah was beside herself with delight. "Does 'this guy' go to my school?"

"Yeah," Jackson said, pleased that she was getting the point without too much work on his part. Out of the corner of his eye, he could see Rico nervously preening himself as he waited to talk to the girl of his dreams.

"And is he maybe not the tallest guy around?" Sarah asked coyly.

Jackson thought for a second. No doubt

about it, Rico *was* height-challenged. Once in a while, Jackson felt some empathy toward the guy, since Jackson was the tiniest bit on the short side himself. "Yeah!" Jackson answered enthusiastically.

"Oh, Jackson!" Sarah squealed. "I like you, too!" She threw her arms around him.

"Huh?" Jackson's eyes widened with shock. He ran back over their conversation in his mind. Okay, yes, he could see how she had gotten the wrong idea. Now, how could he break the bad news to her? "No, I—"

But before he could explain the mistake, he glanced over at Rico, who had watched the scene unfold. And he did *not* look happy.

Rico ripped the fake mustache off his upper lip in despair.

"Ow!" he cried out, his eyes watering. Then he stomped away.

Jackson let out a sigh. This was definitely not how the plan was supposed to go!

Chapter Four

The next day, Miley and Lilly headed into school. Mr. Corelli, one of their teachers, was trying to get the attention of the freshman class.

"Okay, okay, all ninth graders listen up!" Mr. Corelli called out. "The circus I hired for the freshman fund-raiser is no longer available."

"Aww . . ." a crowd of students groaned.

"But no worries," he explained. "One of

our very own has come up with a brilliant, last-minute substitution."

In the crowd, Amber Addison, one of the most ambitious and aggressive students in the class, lit up with excitement. "Karaoke night!" she sang out happily.

Ashley Dewitt, Amber's enthusiastic best friend, tried to lead the crowd of students in a round of applause. Some people clapped, but the response was halfhearted at best. Most of the students knew it would be an opportunity for Amber to hog the spotlight—as usual.

Mr. Corelli and Amber walked down the stairs. She was still focused on the idea of a karaoke night. It would give her an opportunity to stand onstage, all eyes on her, for the entire length of a song. Or maybe several songs. Back to back. Amber *really* liked karaoke.

"For admission, you get food, drink, and the chance to get up there and be compared to"— she sang out the last word—"*me. . . .*"

As a teacher, Mr. Corelli thought it was his duty to encourage his students. But even he came close to rolling his eyes at this. "They get it," he told her.

Amber crossed her arms and glared at him. No one *ever* interrupted her.

"Well, now, I know not all of us can sing as well as some people," Mr. Corelli began. Amber and Ashley pointed to each other to show everyone they knew who their teacher was referring to.

"Stop pointing," Mr. Corelli told them. He turned back to address the crowd. "But I still expect to see everybody here and singing on Saturday night!"

Despite his peppy tone, no one seemed too fired up. In fact, they groaned and muttered to each other. Getting up onstage? In front of all their classmates? And *singing*? It was a recipe for disaster—not to mention having to listen to Amber and Ashley all night!

Just then, Amber caught sight of Miley in the crowd. A mischievous smile spread across her face. Amber and Ashley liked to pick on people, and Miley and Lilly had been their targets for months.

"Hey, Miley," Amber called out. "If you're too gutless to sing, you can always go up there and do one of your pig calls."

"Oh, you mean like this?" Miley retorted. "'Amber, Ashley, get in here!'" She made a few pig snorts.

"Boo-ya!" Lilly cheered, giving Miley a high five. A few other students gathered around to watch the scene that was unfolding.

Ashley frowned, puzzled at Miley's

response. "That's weird. Her pigs have *our* names." Then she realized that the joke was on her. "Oh, *real* mature," she said sarcastically.

"Exactly what we'd expect from the tone-deaf twins!" Amber added with a smirk.

"In your face!" Amber and Ashley yelled in unison. "Ooh!" They turned to walk away, satisfied that they had just won this little battle.

But Lilly couldn't let them off the hook just yet. She was too mad about their insults. She had to say something.

And before Miley could stop her, Lilly cried out, "Well, what you don't know is that I happen to have a *really* great voice."

"What?" Miley blurted out, horrified. "No! Lilly, you can't sing . . ."

Lilly looked confused.

". . . up there, with Amber!" Miley finished quickly.

"Why not?" Lilly asked.

"Because I'm coming down with something and . . ." Miley coughed. "I just gave it to you. Sorry."

"Oh, you two are coming down with something all right," Amber sneered. "*Chicken* pox."

"Emphasis on the *chicken*!" Ashley added, just in case they didn't get the point.

Amber gave her friend an exasperated look. Why was Ashley always explaining her jokes? "*I* put the emphasis on the chicken!" she complained.

"What are you so worried about?" Lilly asked Miley. "You heard that CD. I can take her!" She called out to Amber, "Hey, check this, Twitney Houston, I'm going to sing you off that stage."

Amber scowled at her. "Oh, it is *so* on! I'll see you Saturday night, Smelly Clarkson!"

Meanwhile, Lilly was gloating to Miley. "This is going to be so great! When she hears my voice, she's going to freak!"

"She ain't the only one, honey," Miley muttered. Oh, boy, Miley thought. This is going to be one interesting evening!

Chapter Five

Later on at the Surf Shack, Jackson was going to try to explain what had happened with Sarah. Here goes nothing, he thought, approaching Rico.

Rico sneered up at him from a stool at the counter. "Well, well, well, if it isn't the Sarah stealer, the babe bandit!" he snapped.

Jackson rolled his eyes. "Look, Rico," he began, "do you really think I want a fourteen-year-old girlfriend whose idea of a date is snuggling around a campfire roasting gluten-free marshmallows?"

"I don't care what you want. All I care about is Sarah and her happiness," Rico said with determination. "That's why I need you to crush her and send her crawling back to me."

Jackson shook his head. "Look, I am not going to break her heart. I'll find another way," Jackson said firmly.

At that moment, Sarah came running up to them, smiling happily. "Hey, Jackson!" she called out. "This weekend, want to go get typhoid shots together?"

"Why would I want to do that?" Jackson asked, puzzled.

"So we don't get typhoid when we go to build alternative housing in Tanzania, you silly goose," she said with a giggle. "'Bye!"

As she ran off, Rico stared sadly after

her. "*I* should be the one risking infectious disease in Tanzania!" he exclaimed.

"No arguments here," Jackson sighed. This girl was crazier than he thought!

Meanwhile, at the Stewart home, Miley was sitting at the piano in her living room and doing her very best to teach Lilly how to sing. Unfortunately, she was discovering that her very best was nowhere near good enough.

Lilly stood next to the piano as Miley played a series of notes.

"La, la, la, la . . ." Lilly sang loudly.

"Try to hit all of the notes . . ." Miley sang in response.

"I'm hitting all of the notes . . ." Lilly sang back, smiling.

Miley sighed. She didn't think Lilly had managed to hit *one* note yet—and the karaoke contest was tomorrow!

"Miley, we've been at this for an hour," Lilly complained. "I don't want to damage my voice."

"Trust me," Miley said dryly, "that isn't going to happen."

"I don't even know why I need to do these stupid exercises," Lilly went on, pouting. "We both know I'm going to blow Amber off the stage."

Miley knew where Lilly was going with this. She had to stop her . . . and fast.

"This isn't about Amber," Miley said. She tried to give Lilly a confident and reassuring smile. "This is about you being the best you can be."

Lilly looked at her in confusion. "But I'm already the best I can be."

"Oh, I hope not," Miley said before she could help herself. She added quickly,

"I mean, there's always room for improvement, right?"

Before Lilly could answer, Mr. Stewart came into the living room. "Hey, Lilly," he said. "How'd your mom like her birthday present?"

"She . . ." Lilly sang the last two words with a big smile, ". . . loved it."

Mr. Stewart gave her a doubtful look. "Did you play it for her or sing it?" he asked as he headed toward the kitchen to get a snack.

Miley followed right behind him. It was definitely time to give her dad an update on the very serious situation they were in.

"She played it, her mom loved it, and now Lilly has challenged Amber to a sing-off in front of the whole ninth grade," she reported rapidly.

"Yep," Lilly said with a satisfied smile. "I'm going to sing 'I Got Nerve.'"

Mr. Stewart raised his eyebrows. "You sure do," he remarked.

Miley gave him a pleading look. "Help me," she whispered.

Her dad did not disappoint her. Immediately, he said, "You know, Lilly, your voice reminds me of another great singer."

Lilly's face lit up. "Really? Who? Beyoncé? Shakira?"

He shook his head and then, very solemnly, said, "Johnny Cash."

"Really?" Lilly giggled. Then she frowned. Wasn't Johnny Cash a *country* singer? And a *guy*? How did she sound like *him*? "Huh?" she asked, now confused.

"Yeah, you just got something really special about your voice," Mr. Stewart went on. "Something honest."

Miley was staring at him with disbelief. "Where're you going with this, cowboy?" she asked out of the corner of her mouth.

"Now, you see, what Johnny does is he talks his songs," Mr. Stewart said, a gleam in his eye.

"Brilliant . . ." Miley practically shouted. Quickly, she added, ". . . ly. He, uh, talks his songs *brilliantly*."

Mr. Stewart recited a few lines of Lilly's song in the spoken-word rhythm that he was referring to.

Miley snuck a peek over at Lilly to see if she was buying this. "Ooh," Miley said about her dad's performance. "Chills."

But not only was Lilly *not* buying this, she was beginning to become suspicious. "Okay, what's going on?" she demanded.

"Nothing!" Miley replied a little too

loudly. She muttered to her dad, "Got anything else?"

He shrugged. "Can she rap?"

"Hello!" Lilly yelled. "Still in the room!"

Miley sighed. "Daddy, maybe it's time that you—"

"Leave?" he said with relief. "If you insist."

"I was going to say 'tell her the truth.' Coward!" Miley called after him as he hurried out of the room. She turned to Lilly and smiled sweetly.

"What truth?" Lilly asked curiously.

Miley sighed. She had to fess up sometime. It might as well be now.

"This . . ." Miley said. She walked to the kitchen counter and pressed PLAY on the stereo.

Suddenly Lilly's actual singing, in all its off-key glory, filled the room.

"What did you do to my voice?" Lilly asked, stunned.

"On this CD, nothing," Miley explained. "On the one you gave your mom . . . a lot."

Lilly gasped as she realized what Miley was saying. "You remixed me?"

"Technology," Miley said with a chuckle, hoping that Lilly would see the humorous side of the situation. "Gotta love it, huh?"

But Lilly was not laughing. "Oh, man, so *this* is how I'm going to sound in front of the whole ninth grade! Thanks a lot!"

She headed for the front door. Miley turned off the stereo and ran after her.

"Lilly! I'm sorry," Miley said sincerely. "I was just trying to do something nice."

"Oh, like what, ruin my life?" Lilly shouted. "If I don't sing, Amber makes a fool out of me and if I *do* sing, *I* make a fool out of me."

"What do you want from me?" Miley asked. "If I could loan you my voice, I would."

The two girls looked at each other. Instantly, they knew that they both had the same idea—and it was brilliant!

"Hit it," Lilly said.

Miley opened her mouth and began to sing. "La, la, la, la . . ."

At the exact same time, Lilly mouthed the words without making a sound. It looked exactly like she was singing—and it sounded like she had a voice as good as Hannah Montana's!

Grinning, Miley stopped singing . . . but Lilly kept going. No words were coming out, but she was so excited that she threw her arms out and opened her mouth even wider. Then she saw Miley staring at her.

"Sorry," Lilly said. "I like to go for a big finish."

"You'll take what I give you," Miley said sternly.

"Yes, m'am," Lilly said.

She'd do anything that Miley told her to, if it meant she could avoid complete humiliation in front of the entire school—and especially in front of Amber and Ashley!

Chapter Six

It was another beautiful day on the beach in Malibu, California. Sarah smiled as she walked across the sand, picking up trash as she went and taking in the beautiful natural environment all around her. The sun, the sea, the birds, the breeze . . .

Then she spotted Jackson in the Surf Shack. She smiled, but her expression suddenly changed to one of shock.

Was he spraying his hair? With a

product that came out of an *aerosol* can? Jackson was nothing more than an environmental vandal!

"Jackson!" she shouted. "Jackson, what are you *doing*?"

"Just locking in perfection, baby," Jackson replied smoothly. "I call it shellacksin' the Jackson."

Her mouth dropped open. Not only was he destroying Mother Earth, but he was mispronouncing the word "shellacking" to rhyme with his name! Sarah loved poetry almost as much as she loved baby seals. She felt a shiver of unease that only got worse as Jackson continued talking.

"Gorgeous and water-resistant to two hundred meters," he said, referring to his hair, which now resembled a helmet.

"But aerosol sprays are ruining our

ozone!" Sarah cried. "Aren't you worried about global warming?"

"So my grandkids will never see a polar bear, big whoop," he said with a shrug. "I never got to see a dinosaur; you don't see me crying about it." He frowned as he shook the spray can. "Oh, man, I'm all out."

He tossed it onto a pile of used aerosol containers. Then he reached under the counter, picked up another can of hairspray, and started spraying his hair again.

Sarah gasped. "You can't just leave those here," she protested. "They have to be properly disposed of in a hazardous-waste facility."

"Oh, I've got a hazardous-waste facility," he answered, hopping over the counter. "I call it the Pacific Ocean."

"But that will pollute our beaches!" she protested.

"I don't care," Jackson said, trying to sound casual. He looked her right in the eye. "Aren't I horrible? You should break up with me."

There, he thought. That ought to do it. Rico, she's all yours. . . .

But Sarah looked at him with sympathy. "Break up with you?" she said. "You need me now more than ever."

Jackson couldn't believe his ears. "What?" he asked in shock.

"This is perfect!" Sarah exclaimed happily. "I was feeling guilty about spending time with you when I could be saving the world, but now by spending time with you, I *will* be saving the world!" She gave him a big hug, then pulled back. "Ow, your hair hurts."

"All right, look," Jackson said. He hated to do this—it was his last resort—but she had left him with no choice. He had to tell her the truth. "I—I don't have a crush on you. I never had a crush on you. When I came to talk to you, I was talking about Rico. *He's* the one who likes you."

Sarah listened intently. She looked over in Rico's direction and frowned. "He doesn't look like he likes me," she said doubtfully.

Jackson turned to see what she was looking at. "Sweet niblets!" he cried.

Rico strolled up to them, his arm slung around the shoulder of a very pretty girl. He had a huge smile on his face.

"Excuse me," Jackson said. "What are you doing?" he asked Rico.

"Chillin' with my new girl, Rrrrrrosalita," Rico said proudly, rolling the *R*s in grand Spanish style.

"But what about Sarrrrrah?" Jackson

asked, rolling a few *R*s right back at him. "You were nuts about her."

"I *was*," Rico agreed. "Until I met Rosalita."

"Sarah!" Jackson insisted, trying to get Rico to come back to his senses.

"Rosalita!" Rico argued.

"Sarah!" Jackson tried again.

"Rosalita!" Rico wasn't budging.

Jackson sighed. He knew when he had lost. He turned back to Sarah. "Look, Sarah, I'm really—"

"It's okay," she said through gritted teeth. "It's obvious you weren't emotionally ready for me."

"Yes!" Jackson cried, his eyes filled with hope. Could it really be this easy? "Yes. Thank you for understanding."

She took a deep breath and tried to center herself. Then she gave him a very sweet smile. "That's why I'll wait."

"Huh?" Jackson asked, a familiar feeling of doom creeping into his stomach. It was the same feeling he got after almost every one of his schemes crashed and burned.

"I waited six years for the California low-flow toilet initiative, and I can wait for you," Sarah said, a serene expression on her face. "'Bye!"

As she gave a little wave and walked away, Jackson made one last attempt to save himself from this situation.

"But I'm not worth waiting for!" he yelled after her. "Ask anybody!"

Chapter Seven

The big moment had finally arrived. The Seaview High School karaoke contest was in full swing . . . and in full *sing*. The quad had been decorated with festive lights. A banner proclaimed that this was: NINTH GRADE KARAOKE NIGHT. A spotlight hit the stage, which had been set up along a row of lockers.

Amber was onstage and giving a fantastic performance. As she followed the lyrics on a karaoke video screen, Oliver operated a soundboard on one side of the stage.

The crowd was bopping along to the music, having a blast. Most of the crowd, that is. Miley and Lilly were huddled in a science classroom, peering through a window that looked out onto the quad. The science teacher had clearly been taking his class through a lesson on spiders: the room was creepily decorated with a large web made out of cargo netting. It featured a number of fake spiders, all neatly labeled with their scientific names. There was even a terrarium that housed a real living and breathing tarantula!

But Miley and Lilly were too focused on practicing their song to pay much attention to science displays. Miley was holding a wireless microphone and listening to Amber intently. Lilly, on the other hand, was listening with a nauseated feeling in the pit of her stomach.

"Oh, man, she sounds good," Lilly said with a sigh.

"Yeah, but you're going to sound better," Miley said confidently. "Oliver's got this mic patched into the same frequency as the stage mic. So I'll be singing in here, your mouth moves out there, and Amber's mouth just does this. . . ." She mimicked Amber's mouth dropping open in astonishment.

"Got it," Lilly said, feeling better. She started to head for the stage, then turned back. "Oh, remember, I like a big finish," she added.

"I remember," Miley said. She shooed her friend away. "Just go and have fun!"

Lilly grinned and dashed out the door.

"Singers," Miley muttered to herself. "They're all divas."

She started to head back to the window, when she suddenly caught sight of that enormous, hairy tarantula.

"Oh!" Miley gasped. "There ain't nothing itsy-bitsy about you, big boy."

Even though the spider was safely contained in the terrarium, Miley moved carefully next to the window. No reason to get any closer than she had to!

Onstage, Amber finished her song with a flourish as the students in the audience cheered. She grinned. "Thank you, thank you. I was good, wasn't I?" she said into the microphone.

Mr. Corelli hurried onto the stage to take the microphone from her. "Ah, that's the always humble Amber Addison!" he announced. He scanned the audience. "All right, who's next?"

Everybody in the crowd glanced around uneasily.

"No way," a few people called out.

"No. Not me," others quickly added.

"Boy, I sure wouldn't want to go up there and sing after someone that wonderful," Ashley said, looking in Lilly's direction. "Who could possibly follow Amber?"

"Ooh, I believe the gauntlet has been thrown down!" Mr. Corelli exclaimed, grinning. "Will Lilly Truscott pick it up?"

Lilly jumped up on the stage. "Give me that mic."

"You've got guts, kid," her teacher said.

"That's not all I've got," Lilly said defiantly. "I've got nerve! Hit it, Oliver!"

Oliver hit a few buttons and the song blasted out of the speakers. Lilly struck a pose and began mouthing the words as Miley did all the singing. Lilly smiled confidently at the thought that no one would actually hear her real voice.

And for a few bars, that was true.

Just as Miley had predicted, Amber was staring at Lilly in shock. "I didn't know she had a voice like that!" she exclaimed.

Ashley was also stunned. "She sounds exactly like—"

"Shut up!" Amber snapped.

"But she's amazing!" Ashley protested. Then she caught sight of Amber's glare and added quickly, "Amazingly *bad*! Ooh!"

Lilly relaxed and started enjoying herself. Sure, she was only lip-synching—but the crowd was really getting into it. She started dancing around a little bit, enjoying the spotlight.

As Miley sang inside the classroom, she

was glad that Lilly was having such a great time onstage. She didn't notice that the tarantula had made its way out of the terrarium—and was now crawling up her leg!

Miley kept singing. The spider kept crawling. Then, right in the middle of a chorus, Miley looked down. . . .

"Spiderrrrr!" she cried.

A terrified yell boomed out of the mic. A look of panic crossed Lilly's face as the audience members glanced at each other in surprise.

Miley kept trying to sing, even though she was seriously freaked out.

First, she tried to flick the spider off her arm, timing her breaths to the rhythm of the song. Confused, Lilly tried desperately to lip-synch her own breathing to match Miley's. It looked odd, to say the least.

Then Miley started spinning around, trying to shake the spider off. Unfortunately, she spun her way right into the web—and got tangled up in the netting! She didn't stop singing, but her voice sounded as if she were about to cry . . . which wasn't far from the truth!

And the spider wasn't giving up! When it got to the top of her head, Miley couldn't keep singing.

"Help me!" she shrieked, before falling to the floor.

A squeal of feedback filled the quad until Oliver finally cut the sound.

Lilly stood still on the stage as everyone stared at her in silence.

"Yeah, you got nerve, all right," Amber said, scoffing at Lilly.

"Just no talent!" Ashley added.

Amber laughed. And then everyone in

the audience joined her and exploded in laughter.

Lilly left the stage, practically in tears. She ran toward the double doors just as Miley came running out of them.

"Lilly!" Miley shouted, catching up with her. "I'm so sorry."

"Come on, let's just get out of here," Lilly grumbled quietly. She was mortified.

But Oliver wasn't going to stand by and watch people make fun of one of his best friends. "Lilly, hold up," he called. Then he turned to address the crowd. "What are you guys laughing at? At least she had the guts to get up there."

Lilly gave him a grateful glance. Oliver really was a good friend.

"Even though she did completely humiliate herself," he added.

"Thank you!" Lilly snapped at him.

She nodded to Miley. "Come on."

"No, Oliver's right," Miley said. Now it was her turn to talk to the other students. "She did humiliate herself."

Lilly couldn't believe this! Were both of her best friends determined to embarrass her even more? "I think they heard it the first time!" she yelled at Miley. "What kind of friend are you?"

Lilly once again headed toward the door. But when she heard Miley say, "The kind I should've been all along," Lilly stopped.

She listened as Miley said to the crowd, "Sure, Lilly doesn't have a great voice. Most of us don't, but does that mean we *shouldn't* sing?"

"Uh, yeah," Amber said, rolling her eyes at how obvious this answer was. She smiled brightly at the audience. "Now who wants to hear me?"

Mr. Corelli spoke into the microphone. "Amber, let's not"—he sang the last word—"*interrupt*." Then he nodded at Miley. "Carry on. I beg you."

Amber tossed her hair angrily, but didn't say anything as Miley continued.

"Singing shouldn't be about showing people up," she said. "It should be about having a great time no matter what you sound like." She walked over to Lilly and gave her an apologetic look. "And I should've known that. Lilly, I'm sorry; I never should've messed with that CD. Your mom would have loved it, just because it came from you."

Lilly hesitated, then smiled. "Yeah, she is a big mush ball," she admitted.

As Miley and Lilly hugged, Mr. Corelli said into the mic, "So, who wants to come up here and have a good time?"

But despite Miley's speech, no one was interested in singing—it was just too intimidating!

"Go up there," Miley said to Lilly. "Show them the *real* Lilly Truscott. I think she's pretty great."

"Thanks," Lilly said, giving her best friend a smile. "Mr. Corelli, I want a do-over."

"You got it," he said, beaming.

As Lilly bounded back onstage, Miley called after her, "Hey, Lilly! Don't forget your big finish."

Lilly grinned and launched into another song. She was still off-key—but she really got the crowd moving! By the end of karaoke night, everyone—from Oliver to Mr. Corelli to Rico—was taking a turn singing their hearts out.

As more and more singers took the stage, Miley and Lilly walked over to where Amber and Ashley were watching in disbelief.

"Congratulations," Lilly said to Amber. "You're the best singer in the school."

"Too bad nobody cares," Miley said.

Miley gave Lilly a high five. This experience had definitely ended on a high note!

Part One

"So, do you think my mom will like it?" Lilly asked Miley after she finished singing.

"I'm fantastic!" Lilly exclaimed. But she didn't know that Miley had remixed the CD!

"I just wish I had someone who could find out if Sarah likes me," Rico told Jackson.

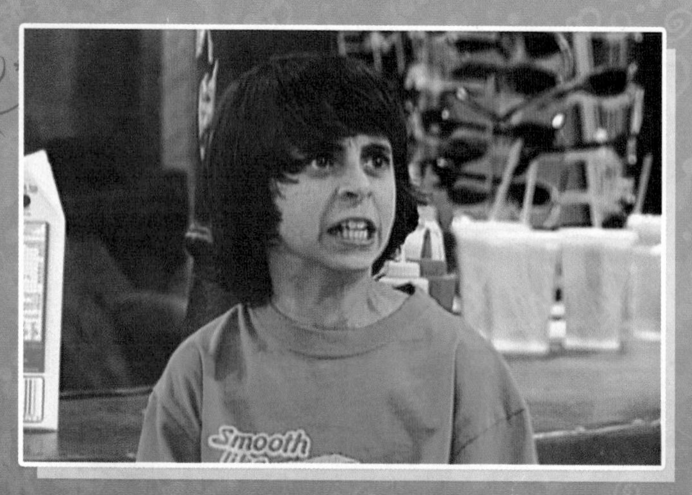

"All I care about is Sarah and her happiness," Rico snarled.

Miley and Lilly looked at each other and knew they had the same idea for the talent show.

"Aren't I horrible? You should break up with me," Jackson told Sarah.

Miley tried to continue lip-synching for Lilly, but there was a giant spider on her arm!

Oliver was even inspired to get up onstage and sing!

Part Two

"Either there was a *Dukes of Hazzard* marathon on last night or you just wrote a new Hannah song," Miley told her dad.

"This song stinks," Miley complained, after reading the song her dad had written.

Jackson and Oliver agreed with Miley. The song was *not* good.

Jackson tried to wake up Miley. She had a habit of sleepwalking when things were bothering her.

"If I fall asleep at home, I'm not going to be able to stop myself from telling Daddy the truth," Miley said.

Miley didn't know what she should do.

Mr. Stewart played Miley the song he had *really* written. She loved it!

The song was a huge hit!

PART TWO

Chapter One

It was morning and Mr. Stewart was already up and making breakfast. As he flipped some eggs with a spatula, he crooned to himself, "Cooking up some eggs, frying them up in a pan, going to add a little cheddar, 'cause I'm a cheesy omelet man."

Miley Stewart and her brother, Jackson, came downstairs just in time to hear the end of their dad's song.

"Good morning, Cheesy Omelet Man," they said in unison.

"Good morning, my loving, beautiful family," Mr. Stewart answered cheerfully.

Miley surveyed the feast he was preparing. "Eggs, bacon," she pointed out. Her eyes brightened. "Either there was a *Dukes of Hazzard* marathon on last night or you just wrote a new Hannah song!"

"Aw, honey, you know me better than that," her father said teasingly. "If I'd written a new song, there would be cinnamon toast."

Just then, the toaster dinged and two slices of cinnamon toast popped up.

"New song!" Miley cheered, rushing over to give her dad a hug.

"Cinnamon toast!" Jackson shouted, equally happy.

"There's nothing like finally cracking a

new song," their dad said with satisfaction.

"I can't wait to hear it!" Miley exclaimed. "Let me go get Lucky Lulu," she said, referring to her dad's fondly nicknamed guitar. She headed for the living room where he usually kept it. Miley looked around. "Where's Lucky Lulu?"

"Lulu's like a lot of older California women," Mr. Stewart said. "She's having some work done on her neck."

Miley shrugged. "That's okay. We can just use, uh, Whammy-Bar Wally," she suggested. She pointed to another guitar. "He's *wone*some," Miley said, making a sad face.

But Mr. Stewart shook his head. "Now, honey, you know I never play you a new song without Lulu. Especially one that could be your biggest hit ever."

"Biggest hit ever?" Miley gasped. She

could hardly contain her excitement. "Okay, you at least have to tell me what it's about. Breaking up? Making up?"

She stopped and gave her dad a warning look. "Please don't let it be another song about my double life. I mean, you might as well tattoo 'I'm really Miley Stewart' on my forehead."

Her dad laughed, but he shook his head. "Sorry, honey, you'll just have to wait. Lulu won't be back until Monday. And I won't be back until after I jog five miles. Matter of fact"—he took a large bite of bacon—"make that five and a half."

Miley smiled at her dad sweetly. "All right, Daddy, whatever you say. I'll wait because you want me to." As he headed out the door, she called after him, "I love you!"

As soon as she was sure he was safely out of earshot, she drew a breath. "All right, where'd that bacon-eating hillbilly hide my song?" She started rooting around the piano, hoping to find it.

Jackson, however, wasn't interested in her new song. He was too focused on his dad's upbeat mood—and, of course, on what that mood meant for him. "Did you see how happy he was?" Jackson asked his sister. "This is great! Now he'll finally let me have another party at the house."

Miley stopped searching for the song long enough to say, "Are you joking? Remember the last time you had a party?"

Of course Jackson remembered. Everyone in Malibu remembered! Although not necessarily for the right reasons.

"Hey, it was one little citywide power outage!" he protested.

"They had to land a jumbo jet on the freeway," Miley reminded him.

"And now those passengers have a great story to tell," Jackson countered.

Miley rolled her eyes and returned to her mission. She picked up her dad's jacket from the piano bench and pulled a folded piece of sheet music from one of the pockets.

"Gotcha!" she cried in triumph.

Jackson was still making his case for why he should be allowed to have a party. As he dialed his cell phone, he said, "Look, I've been begging for months and all I've heard was"—he imitated his dad's voice—"can't talk, got to finish the song. Can't talk, got to finish the song."

As he waited for his call to be answered, Jackson switched back to his own voice. "Well, he's finished the song, he's in a great mood, which means—"

Suddenly, he spoke loudly into the phone. "Max, the party animal is *back*!

Saturday night, my house!"

Having delivered the good news, Jackson hung up, grinning.

Miley's smile, however, had vanished. She stared at the sheet music in shock. "This is awful," she said.

"So, are we smelling a hit?" Jackson asked cheerfully.

Miley shook her head in dismay. "I'm smelling something, but I'm not sure it's a hit. This song stinks!"

Jackson's face fell as he thought about what effect this bad news might have on his party. "Oh, no," he said seriously.

"Oh, yes." Miley held the music under his nose. "Take a whiff."

Chapter Two

Miley sat at the piano, her shoulders drooping, and played the melody of the new song her father had written for her. She was trying to stay optimistic, but she looked anguished as she sang the words:

Dang flabbit, where's that rabbit
He's got a habit of running away
Hey, honey, where's that bunny
He took my money, that ain't okay

Hey, hey, hey, bunn-ay

She had called her best friends, Lilly Truscott and Oliver Oken, to tell them about this very serious situation and they had rushed right over. Now they were listening to her sing with identical looks of horror on their faces.

Still, Lilly tried to sound encouraging. "Well, it certainly . . . rhymes."

Oliver nodded. "With a good band . . ." he began to suggest.

Jackson bobbed his head up and down in agreement. "Good band," he repeated enthusiastically.

He would say anything to get Miley to like this song. If she didn't, Jackson knew that their dad would be back in a funk . . . and he could forget about having a party ever again!

"Some backup vocals . . ." Oliver went on. He looked over at Jackson.

"Backup vocals!" Jackson cried brightly, echoing Oliver again.

Miley shook her head. She knew they were trying to cheer her up, but it wasn't changing the fact that the song was bad. *Really* bad.

"And it'll still be a song about bunnies!" she wailed.

"Which *could* become an Easter classic," Oliver pointed out.

"*Classic,*" Jackson said persuasively.

"This is horrible," Miley groaned. "I've never hated one of his songs before. How am I going to tell him?"

"Maybe you won't have to," Jackson said, trying to sound positive. "I mean, maybe he'll think about it, realize that it's horrible and then fix it before he shows it to you."

Just then, Mr. Stewart came into the house from the deck. He had just returned from his run and was carrying a newspaper he'd picked up while he was out. "Hey, everybody!" he called out.

Miley quickly hid the sheet music.

"Hey, Daddy!" she exclaimed.

Lilly, Oliver, and Jackson all started talking at once to cover up what they had been discussing. "Hey. Hi. What's up?" they said. "How's it going?"

Miley shot them all an exasperated look. When they finally fell silent, she turned back to her dad. "So, Daddy, how was your jog?"

"It was great," he answered, taking a deep breath. "But I keep thinking about that new song."

"Really?" Miley asked, her voice full of hope.

"What song?" Lilly asked, trying to sound innocent.

Oliver picked up on what Lilly was trying to do and decided to help out. Of course, being Oliver, he went completely overboard.

"Oh, you wrote a song? Who knew? Interesting." He paused thoughtfully. Then he blurted out one word: "Easter."

Miley and Lilly both elbowed him.

He jumped and started babbling on, trying to save the moment.

"Uh, island," he said quickly. "Easter Island. Uh, we're studying it at school. Big statues. Nobody knows how they got there. Weird."

"Yeah, really weird!" Lilly jumped in. "So, so strange."

Mr. Stewart looked from Lilly to Oliver, then shrugged. "I would ask what's going on, but then you'd tell me. And why would I want that?"

Miley decided it was time to ease her dad back to a more important topic of conversation.

"So, Daddy, uh, you were thinking about the song?" she said casually. "Nothing wrong with that, just, uh, keep on thinking!" Then she gave him a serious look. "Please," she added.

Her father walked over to the refrigerator to get a drink. "Yeah, well, you know how sometimes you write something and then you take another look at it later and it's not as good as you thought?"

Miley's eyes lit up. "Yeah?"

He grinned. "Well, this isn't one of those times!" he exclaimed.

Her face dropped. "It *isn't*? Are you *sure*?"

"Oh, I'm sure," he answered happily. "I mean, this song is great! And I can't wait to see the look on your face when I play it for you on Monday."

And with that, he headed out of the room. Once he was gone, Miley shared a look of dismay with her friends and her brother.

"What are you going to do?" Oliver asked Miley.

"Stick my head in the freezer," Miley groaned. "Please defrost me when you find a cure for this song."

Jackson decided it was time to step in. "I will tell you what she's going to do, all right? She's going to tell him she loves it. Why? Because she's a wonderful daughter who doesn't want to break her father's heart."

Miley, Lilly, and Oliver all gave him a skeptical look.

"This is still about your party, right?" Lilly asked.

Jackson threw up his hands in exasperation. "Look, Max has already invited fifty people and reserved a deli platter in my name!"

"I can't believe I'm saying this, but Jackson's right," Miley said, flopping down on the couch. She thought about how happy her dad was about the new song. "He's worked so hard on this song and he's so proud of it. I've *got* to tell him I love it."

Lilly and Oliver nodded. They knew Miley was right—but they also knew how hard it was for her to sing something she hated.

"You know what, Miley, it'll be okay," Oliver said encouragingly. "So Hannah sings one clunker. Big deal."

"Yeah, and the video will be cute," Lilly

said, sitting down next to Miley. "You, surrounded by giant, dancing bunnies. Right?" She sang a line of the song in the happiest voice possible. "'I'm the bunny who stole your money. Ooh, ooh.'"

Miley shot her a look, and Lilly stopped singing. "I'm not helping, am I?" she asked.

"No," Miley answered.

Jackson took the seat on the other side of Miley and put his arm around her. "Miles, if it makes you feel any better, I know this is kind of hard on you . . ." he began in a very un-Jackson-like way. Then he reverted to his old self. ". . . but my life . . . is so good right now! Boo-ya!" he yelled, racing upstairs.

Miley sighed. How was she going to get herself out of this one?

Chapter Three

That night, Miley had a hard time falling asleep. She kept worrying about the song and if—or worse, *how*—she would tell her dad what she really thought about it. And even after she finally nodded off, her sleep was restless.

She started mumbling to herself in her sleep. "Got to tell Dad," she muttered. "Got to tell Dad."

After a few moments, she stumbled to

her feet, still asleep, and walked toward her bedroom door. "Dad," she mumbled. "Got to tell Dad."

Downstairs, Jackson was sitting on the couch, watching TV.

"Dad?" Miley asked in a dazed voice as she wandered down the stairs to the living room. "Dad?"

"Where's Dad?" Miley asked her brother.

"He's still on his date," Jackson replied.

"Have to tell him the truth," she said, sounding zombielike.

"What?" Jackson asked, giving Miley a strange look.

She headed for the front door. "Have to tell him the truth," she repeated.

She opened the door and stepped outside.

"No. Wait, what are you—" Jackson

dashed after her. "Miles, what are you doing?"

"Hate that song," she grumbled. "Hate that song."

Then Jackson realized what was happening. "Oh, man. Are you sleepwalking?"

Suddenly, Miley fell back into such a deep sleep that walking was no longer an option. She toppled over into Jackson's arms.

"I'll take that as a yes." He grunted as he carried her back inside the house. "Oh, sorry," he said when he accidentally bumped her as he struggled to get her to the couch. Once she was lying down, he tried to rouse her. "Come on, Miles. Miley, wake up. Come on, Miley, wakey, wakey."

Suddenly, Jackson heard a car door slam outside. He raised his head in alarm. "Oh, no," he said. "Dad."

That seemed to get Miley's attention. She began sleep-talking again. "Dad? Hate that song. Got to tell Dad."

"Uh, no, no, no," Jackson said quickly, panicked at the notion. Then he had an idea. "Of course you do," he said, agreeing. "I'll take you to him. He's right under here!"

He threw a blanket over Miley. "No way you're blowing my party," he said, and threw her over his shoulder.

He was hurrying up the stairs with his sleeping sister when Mr. Stewart came into the house.

"Jackson, what in the world?" Mr. Stewart asked incredulously when he saw what was going on.

"Shh!" Jackson whispered. "Miley sleeping, Jackson helping"—he winced as the strain of carrying his sister suddenly got to him—"thigh cramping."

Mr. Stewart just shook his head. His kids definitely kept him on his toes!

A few minutes later, Miley was in bed again, fast asleep. Suddenly, her eyes snapped open. "Got to tell Dad. Got to tell Dad. Got to tell—"

She stepped out of the bed and crashed to the floor. Now wide awake, she looked around in confusion as to what had just happened. Then she noticed Jackson, who was sleeping on her bedroom floor. She had just stumbled over *him*!

"Jackson, what are you doing?" she asked.

He looked at her sleepily. "First of all, do you want to tell Dad the truth?"

"No, of course not!" Miley answered, astonished.

"Good," he said with relief. "You're awake."

Miley let out a deep breath. "Now that we've covered the obvious, what are you doing here?"

"You were sleepwalking and you almost told Dad that you hate his song," Jackson explained.

But Miley had been tricked by Jackson too many times in the past to fall for that! "Yeah, right," she scoffed.

Jackson raised an eyebrow. "You think some guy named Jimmy in your biology class is"—he spoke in a high-pitched voice—"'yum-alicious.'"

Miley gasped. "How do you know that?"

"You told me that an hour ago!" Jackson exclaimed, proving his point. "Look, this is just like that time you were five and you lied about breaking Mom's favorite vase.

Remember? You felt so guilty, you started sleepwalking and blabbing the truth about everything."

Miley paled as the horrible memory came back to her.

"You are not going to blow my party," her brother said firmly.

"Hey, I'm doing the best I can!" she protested.

"Now you're going to do the best that *I* can," he answered. Jackson was set on having his party, and he wasn't going to let anyone stand in the way!

Sure enough, Miley hadn't been sleeping for very long before she opened her eyes, got out of bed, and headed for the staircase once again. This time, though, Jackson was prepared. He had tied a fishing line around his sister's waist, and he was sleeping in a chair, holding on to the fishing rod *very* tightly.

As soon as Miley started to move, the line pulled on a bell attached to the fishing rod, making it jingle.

Jackson woke up with a start and pulled on the fishing rod. Miley was safely yanked back into her bedroom.

But the noise disturbed Mr. Stewart as he dozed on the living room couch. He stirred, then opened his eyes, wondering if he had heard something. After a few moments, he went back to sleep, muttering to himself. Apparently, Miley wasn't the only Stewart who had a sleep-talking problem!

Chapter Four

A few days later, Miley sat in a classroom with her head in her hands, completely exhausted. Class hadn't started yet, and Miley was already falling asleep. Lilly and Oliver stood next to Miley's desk, looking at her with concern.

"Miley, you haven't slept in two days," Lilly said. "You can't keep doing this. You've got to get some rest."

"I know," Miley said with a sigh. "But if

I fall asleep at home I'm not going to be able to stop myself from telling Daddy the truth. And if I fall asleep anywhere else, who knows what's going to spill out of my mouth!"

Miley let out a huge yawn. Oliver recoiled. "Whoa!" he said. "Speaking of something spilling out of your mouth, somebody forgot to brush this morning."

"Hey, what do you want from me?" Miley snapped. "I'm amazed I could even get myself dressed."

"Wow, she *is* tired," Oliver said to Lilly.

"Yeah, I know," Lilly replied. Then an idea struck her. "Hey, she can sleep over at my house tonight. Hey, Miley, you can . . . Miley?"

Miley was slumped over her desk, fast asleep.

Just then, their teacher, Ms. Kunkle,

entered the room. "Good morning, class," she said briskly.

Oliver's eyes widened with alarm. Ms. Kunkle was known throughout Seaview High School—throughout the entire school district, in fact—for being a very strict teacher. She got mad when she caught a student daydreaming, let alone one who was *actually* dreaming.

"Uh, Kunkle!" he blurted out as a warning. Ms. Kunkle's laser-beam gaze swung over in his direction. "Uh, comma Ms.," he said, trying to recover. He pointed to himself. "Oken comma Oliver." He pointed to Lilly. "Truscott comma Lilly."

"Don't drag me into this," Lilly said immediately, glaring at Oliver.

Ms. Kunkle gave them a cold stare and walked to the front of the room to write on the blackboard. As soon as her back was turned, Lilly and Oliver sprang into action. They propped Miley's elbows on the desk with her chin in her hands. She was still fast asleep.

As they took their seats, Lilly whispered, "Miley. Miley, wake up. Wake up!"

Ms. Kunkle spun around. "Who's talking?" she demanded.

Miley's eyes suddenly opened, but she had the dazed look of a sleepwalker. "*You* are, Skunkle," she said. "In that awful prison warden voice of yours. It is torture."

"Yikes," Lilly remarked softly. It was bad enough Miley had been sleeping . . . now she was sleep-talking! And who knew what she might say!

The class turned to stare at Miley, who was calmly looking at Ms. Kunkle.

"Excuse me. What did you say?" the stunned teacher managed to spit out.

"She said your voice sounds like a prison warden," Rico offered helpfully. "Oh, and it's torture."

"I heard her," Ms. Kunkle snipped.

Rico shrugged. "Just trying to help."

"What you need is to stop borrowing your grandmother's clothes," Miley went on.

"Hey-o!" Rico exclaimed, showing his appreciation of Miley's creativity.

"Wait!" Lilly cried. "No, no, no. She doesn't mean it. She's sleepwalking."

Oliver nodded vigorously. "And when she sleepwalks she can only tell the truth," he added.

"Truth," Miley muttered. "Got to tell Dad the truth."

"Whoa!" Lilly shouted, hoping to stop Miley's babbling. She reached over to grab her friend, then said pleadingly to Ms. Kunkle, "I mean, look at her. She'd never talk to you like that if she was awake. She'd lie and say you look nice."

Then Lilly realized that what she had just said was *not* going to help . . . but it was too late. She smiled at Ms. Kunkle. "Hey, great top."

Miley chose that moment to rejoin the conversation. "Last time she wore it, you said that if you polished a table with it, the table would punch you in the face," she responded to Lilly, accidentally outing her friend.

"I was kidding," Lilly said, chuckling nervously. "Tables can't punch." She leaned in closer to Miley. "Wake up!" she shouted.

Ms. Kunkle frowned. "Stewart, are you really asleep?"

"Are you really wearing those shoes?" Miley asked.

"Hey-o!" Rico said again.

"They're comfortable and I walk to work!" Ms. Kunkle protested.

"Why?" Miley asked. "Broom in the shop?"

Oliver couldn't help it. He burst out laughing. The image of Ms. Kunkle as a witch was just too funny.

But when Ms. Kunkle glared at him, Oliver cleared his throat and turned serious. "I'm laughing because it's so ridiculous. You're—you're a lovely woman and I'm surprised you haven't been married yet," he said, sinking a little farther down in his seat.

"Yesterday you said it was because of her man hands," Miley offered, holding up her own hands.

"Soft, supple man hands is what—is what I meant," Oliver stammered. He paused, then added soulfully, "Would you marry me, Karen?"

"All right, knock it off," the teacher snarled. "You're not all asleep."

"That's because you haven't started teaching yet," Miley responded.

"Oh," Oliver groaned.

"Okay, that's enough," Ms. Kunkle said, glaring at Miley.

Miley smiled back pleasantly, then closed her eyes and fell back asleep right against Lilly. She even started snoring a little. Lilly struggled to stand her up. As she heaved Miley to her feet, Miley finally woke up.

Then she looked around and found everyone in the class staring at her. She groaned. "Sorry. Where were we?"

Ms. Kunkle thought it was about time for a snappy one-liner of her own. "Well, we're in science class, and you're in trouble," she said. "Principal's office. Now."

As Miley gathered her books, she murmured to Lilly, "How bad was it?"

Lilly said, "Well, it started with 'Skunkle' . . ."

". . . and made it all the way down to 'man hands,'" Oliver finished. "Thank you very much."

Miley bit her lip in embarrassment. "I'm thinking it's time to tell my daddy the truth," she said slowly.

"You think?" Oliver and Lilly said in unison.

Chapter Five

Later that day, Jackson was hanging out at the Surf Shack with some friends and feeling pretty good. He'd hosted some legendary blowouts in the past, but tonight's party was going to take *awesome* to a whole new level! And now that the word was out that the Stewarts' house was going to be rockin', *everyone* wanted to come. Jackson knew he had to make sure he kept the guest list under control.

"Yo, Jackson," a voice said behind him. "I'm bringing a few extra people to your party."

Jackson rolled his eyes. Here we go, he thought.

"Sorry, dude, there's no—" Jackson began to say as he turned around. Then he saw the enormous, muscled guy standing behind him. It was Wayne, who was known throughout the school for being a bully.

"Hey," Jackson said with a gulp. "Yeah, dude, of course. Bring whoever you want. Uh, by the way, love the T-shirt." He leaned in closer and read its slogan out loud. IF YOU CAN READ THIS YOU'RE ABOUT TO BE HIT.

That was enough warning for Jackson! He jumped out of the way, truly frightened.

Wayne laughed. "You're a funny little dude," he said.

"Thanks, man," Jackson said, breathing a sigh of relief.

"But if your party stinks, I'm going to rearrange your face," Wayne added in a menacing tone.

"As well you should," Jackson replied weakly.

Once Wayne was safely gone, Jackson's friend Max walked over to where Jackson was standing. "Dude, I cannot *believe* the buzz on this party!" Max said. "Girls are saying 'hi' to me just because I know you! How did you get your dad to say yes to this?"

Jackson shifted his feet nervously. "Well, as you know, it's just a matter of psychology, timing, and a little sprinkle—"

"And you haven't asked him yet, have you?" Max interrupted, giving Jackson a knowing look.

"Okay, technically, no," Jackson admitted. "But I'm on my way to ask him right now. And trust me, he's going to be in a great mood."

Max shook his head. "He better be," he warned Jackson. "You cancel this party, you're going to spend the rest of high school eating lunch with the Chess Club! You know how many cute girls are in the Chess Club? Zero."

"Well, I thought your girlfriend was in the Chess Club," Jackson said, nodding toward a girl sitting on the beach. She was wearing a CHESS ROCKS T-shirt.

When she saw them looking in her direction, she waved. Jackson and Max politely waved back, but Max's smile looked forced.

"That's why I need this party," he said under his breath to Jackson. "Really, really badly."

Jackson nodded, even as he and Max kept smiling and waving at Max's girlfriend. He knew the stakes were high, and he was determined to throw a party that would go down in history!

When Jackson got home, he walked into the kitchen. He was a little nervous about approaching his dad to ask about the party, but he thought he had really mastered the art of persuasion in recent years—especially if he did a little buttering up first.

"Dad?" he called out.

"Just out of the shower!" Mr. Stewart yelled out from upstairs. "Down in a few!"

"You take your time, you brilliant songwriter," Jackson shouted back. It was never too soon to start the buttering-up process. In fact, maybe he should lay it on a little thicker. "You hero and role model," he added.

But Mr. Stewart knew his son well. "Whatever you broke, fix it or bury it in the yard," he called out as he turned on a hair dryer.

Then Jackson spied Lucky Lulu, his dad's favorite guitar, back on its stand. "Yes! Yes!" he exclaimed to himself, excited. "He's got Lucky Lulu back, he's blow-drying. It's a perfect storm of Dad happiness!"

Miley walked in the door, looking tired and frazzled. "Dad," she called out. "Dad, I have to talk to you."

Jackson's gleeful expression suddenly turned to one of panic. "Oh, no, here we go again!" he yelled. "Miley, stop!"

"Jackson, I'm sorry about your party, but I can't do this anymore," Miley said.

"I've got to tell Daddy the truth."

"No!" he shouted. "No, no, no, you don't! You're just sleepwalking! Come on, Miles, ups-a-daisy!" He snapped his fingers in her face.

"Stop that!" Miley demanded. "Stop it. I'm awake!"

"Of course you are," her brother said calmly. "Now, come here."

He guided her into the kitchen.

"Jackson—" Miley began to protest. Now that she had decided to tell her father the truth, she wanted to get it over with as quickly as possible.

Jackson didn't let her finish. "Look, I know you're supposed to wake a sleep-walker gently, but you leave me no choice," he said. "Desperate times call for loud cookware."

He grabbed two frying pans and banged

them together several times in front of her face—*loudly*.

Miley stared at him for a moment. "I'm still awake and *you're* still an idiot," she said, annoyed.

Just then, their father's voice floated down from the upstairs bathroom. "What the heck is going on down there?"

This was her opening! Miley called back, "Daddy, I—"

"Nothing!" Jackson interrupted loudly. "Nothing, nothing. We're just cooking you dinner, handsome! Keep working on the 'do, we'll see you in a few!"

He leaned close and said, right into Miley's ear, "Please, please, please, wake up!"

She pulled back with a grimace. "I'm still awake, you're still an idiot, and now my ear is full of spit."

"Sorry," he said. "Let me rinse it out for you." He grabbed a pitcher from the counter and threw water in Miley's face. She gasped with shock, then grabbed him by the nose.

"Do you believe I'm awake now?" she asked dangerously.

"Yes," Jackson said, his voice somewhat strained because of her grip on his nose. "I do."

Miley let go. "Listen, Jackson. Awake or asleep, I'm still telling Dad the truth."

"No, you can't!" Jackson cried. "Look, my reputation and the current arrangement of my face depend on it," he said, thinking of Wayne.

"Maybe next time your face shouldn't throw a party without getting permission first!" Miley said, exasperated. "Listen, Jackson, I'm sorry, but I respect Dad too much to lie to him."

Mr. Stewart was walking down the stairs just as Miley finished her sentence. When he heard this, he stopped on the landing. Miley's back was to him, so she didn't see him, but Jackson did.

"Miley—" Jackson said in a warning tone.

Miley thought Jackson was still trying to keep her from talking to her dad. "No!" she said firmly. "Jackson, this song is a joke. It's embarrassing. And no matter how much it hurts, I have to tell him that I found it and it's the worst song he's ever written."

"Miley!" Jackson raised his voice, hoping that would stop her.

But she kept going. "It may be the worst song *ever* written."

Suddenly, Miley sensed that someone else was in the room, and she finally picked up on what Jackson had been trying to tell her. She turned to see her father. "I did say '*may* be,'" she added weakly.

"I heard it," Mr. Stewart said, shocked at what he had just overheard. "I just can't believe it."

And with that, he walked out onto the deck. Oh, no, Miley thought. This wasn't the way I wanted to break the news to him at all!

Chapter Six

Miley walked onto the deck and saw her dad sitting on the steps, staring out at the ocean. She went over to sit beside him.

"Dad, do you hate me?" she asked.

He smiled slightly. "No, of course I don't hate you," he said. "I hate it that you hate the song, because I was just so sure you'd love it."

"You were?" Miley asked, amazed. Then she caught herself. This was a sensitive moment; she shouldn't sound quite so flabbergasted. "I mean . . ." she began. But it was no use, she couldn't hide her astonishment. She finished in exactly the same voice, "You *were?*"

Mr. Stewart shrugged, looking as puzzled as she felt. "I don't get it," he said. "You've never hated one of my songs before." He sighed. "I suppose I could take another look at it. What was it that bothered you? The music? The lyrics? The message?"

"What message?" Miley asked. "'Dang flabbit, where's my rabbit? He took my money.' What are you trying to say, bunnies can't be trusted?"

To Miley's shock, her dad started laughing.

"Dad, this isn't funny!" she protested. "Come on, kids don't want to hear that stuff. They love bunnies!"

Still chuckling, he said, "Yeah, and so did

you when you were five years old." He turned to look at her. "That's when you wrote that song."

Miley did a double take. "Bunny man say *what*?"

"Well, actually you came up with the words, but I wrote it down for you," Mr. Stewart said.

"What was it doing in your pocket?" Miley asked, still shocked.

"I keep it with me for when I get stuck," he explained. "Gives me a little bit of inspiration . . . and a giggle every now and then. Kind of reminds me of the good old days." He sighed as he stared off at the ocean, lost in memories for a moment, then looked at her. "You would have known that if you had just asked."

Miley couldn't believe it! Everything she'd gone through—keeping a secret, sleepwalking because she was keeping a secret, being sent to the principal's office because she was sleepwalking because she was keeping a secret—it all could have been avoided if she'd been honest with her dad from the beginning. Then something occurred to her. "Wait a minute. You mean there's a *good* song?"

Mr. Stewart got up and headed toward the house. "There sure is. You want to hear it?"

She grinned. "Do bunnies steal money?"

When they went into the living room, they found Jackson holding out Lucky Lulu.

"I am loving it already!" Jackson exclaimed.

"You haven't even heard it, son," Mr. Stewart said as he took the guitar, sat down on the couch, and pulled a piece of sheet music from his pocket.

"Sure, I have," Jackson said. He pointed to his heart and said earnestly, "In here."

Miley stood behind her dad and whispered to herself. "Please be good, please be good, please be good," she pleaded.

Mr. Stewart overheard her and glanced over his shoulder. Caught, Miley stopped talking, smiled, and gave him a big thumbs-up.

"All right, here goes," he said.

Miley kept her fingers crossed behind her back.

As he sang the first chorus, Miley and Jackson looked at each other and smiled. The song was good. *Really*, really good.

Miley sat on the couch next to her dad and began singing along, feeling happier than she had in days.

A few weeks later, as Miley and her dad sat

on the couch once again, Miley felt even more cheerful than before. This time, they were watching a tape of her performing the song as Hannah Montana. The audience erupted into applause when she finished.

On the TV screen, Hannah smiled and waved to the crowd.

On the couch, Miley said, “Thanks, Daddy.”

Her dad smiled at her. “My pleasure, bud.”

Chapter Seven

Jackson finally had his party and—as he had hoped—it was epic.

As one of the guests walked out the front door, he said to Jackson, "That was great, dude."

"Well, thanks for coming!" Jackson said brightly. He called out to other guests who were heading for their cars, "Glad you guys had a good time. Especially you, Wayne! Watch out for that branch!"

He winced at the sound of a loud crack. "Or, just ignore it and walk right through it," he added. "Who needs a helmet, huh?"

He closed the door and looked around the living room, which was a complete mess. "Whoa! In the light it looks a lot worse," he commented.

His dad was surveying the disaster area as well. "Well, that's okay, son," he said. "I'll just call the maid service."

Jackson brightened. "Well, thanks, Dad! You know that is one of the many reasons why you're still my hero, my role model, my—" Jackson was saying when he was interrupted by the ringing of his cell phone. "Just a second. Hello?"

"Clean it up!" Mr. Stewart yelled into his own phone.

Jackson had a feeling he'd be picking up trash and washing dishes for the next few hours, but he still gave it his best shot. "Who is this? I think you've got the wrong number. Don't call here anymore," he said, and hung up the phone.

Put your hands together for the next Hannah Montana book . . .

Hit or Miss

Adapted by Laurie McElroy

Based on the series created by Michael Poryes and Rich Correll & Barry O'Brien

Based on the episode, "Me And Mr. Jonas And Mr. Jonas And Mr. Jonas," Written by Douglas Lieblein

Miley Stewart drummed her fingers against the wall and let out a big sigh. She was dressed as Hannah Montana in the hallway of a recording studio. The red neon sign above the studio door was lit. A sign on the door read: Do Not Enter When the

Red Light Is On. Whoever was in the studio was eating into her recording time, and she was getting impatient. She stood up and paced the hall, frowning.

Miley's father, Robby Ray Stewart, wasn't nearly as worked up. He was doing a crossword puzzle to pass the time. "Five-letter word: sixth president of the United States," he said.

Instead of answering, Miley groaned.

"That would work if his name was John Quincy *Ugh,*" her father joked.

Miley shook her head. "Dad, I need to record now! What is taking so long?" she demanded. "Hannah is in the zone."

Hannah Montana was Miley Stewart's alter ego. By day, Miley was just like any other high-school girl. By night, she was pop-music sensation Hannah Montana. Miley loved being Hannah onstage.

Offstage, she wanted to be able to hang with her friends, go to school, and to the mall. Miley wanted people to like her for who she was, and not just because she was famous.

In order to do that, she kept her Hannah Montana identity a secret. When she was Hannah, Miley covered her long, brown, wavy hair with a blond wig, and traded in her t-shirt and jeans for glamorous sequins and leather jackets.

Mr. Stewart was Hannah's songwriter and manager. He wore a disguise, too—a mustache and a hat. He knew his daughter well enough to recognize the real reason for her impatience. It had nothing to do with being in the zone, and *everything* to do with shopping.

"So what time is that big shoe sale you're meeting Lilly at?" he asked.

"Three-thirty," Miley admitted. "And you know all the sixes go first!"

"No, honey, I'm proud to say I don't know that," Mr. Stewart told her. "Now what you need to do is just relax. Whoever is in there is just running a little late. They'll be done any minute."

Miley didn't want to relax. She wanted to record her song and get to that shoe sale. "They'll be done sooner than a minute," she said, grabbing the door handle.

"Hey!" Mr. Stewart yelled, trying to stop her.

But he was too late. Miley had opened the door and marched into the recording studio.

A sound technician sat behind a panel of recording equipment. Three guys sat in a soundproof booth behind a glass window, putting the finishing touches on a song.

"Okay, who do you think you are?" Miley yelled, "The—"

She stopped short when she saw who was recording. She recognized their faces. "Sweet mama!" she exclaimed. "It's the Jonas Brothers!"

The Stewarts had moved from Tennessee to a beach house in Malibu, California, a few years ago, but that didn't stop Miley from lapsing into a Tennessee twang when she was surprised. Miley might have been a teen superstar, but she was also a teenage girl—*and* a big fan.

Kevin, Joe, and Nick Jonas were staring through the glass at her, wondering why she had interrupted their recording session.

Miley quickly pulled herself together and tried to act as if she wasn't the one who had barged into a recording session. "Daddy, I told you somebody was in here," she said over her shoulder. Then she flipped a switch on the soundboard so the guys could hear her. "I am so sorry, guys. He gets so impatient."

Mr. Stewart walked in, rolling his eyes. "Sorry, fellas, I've got a big shoe sale I need to get to," he said wryly.

Nick Jonas hit his brother Joe on the arm. "Dudes, it's Hannah Montana!" he exclaimed.